A COFFIN OF CLEAR WATER

In a small village in the south-east corner of France a coffin of white marble containing the bones of two early-Christian martyrs gives forth a steady supply of clear water. Every year hundreds of people flock to the abbey church to obtain some water, convinced of its miraculous nature and ability to cure them of illness.

Here the author traces the history of the coffin and looks at the theories which scientists have put forward to explain this eight-hundred-year-old enigma.

A COFFIN OF CLEAR WATER

Anthony Fitzherbert

ARTHUR H. STOCKWELL LTD.
Elms Court   Ilfracombe
Devon

Colour Illustrations set between pages 32-37

ISBN 0 7223 2394-8

Printed in Great Britain by
Arthur H. Stockwell Ltd.
Elms Court   Ilfracombe
Devon

CONTENTS

PROLOGUE

"Condensation" said the expert "can not produce three gallons of water a week from a coffin."

A lifetime's experience as a Royal Engineer made it easy for me to agree with him!

"Everyone knows" I said, "that water comes from the sky; from the atmosphere; from the ground and even from some plants too, but I have never heard that it comes in quantity from empty (?) marble coffins." I looked at the expert: "Where's it coming from then?"

"Don't ask me" he replied, "it's a complete mystery."

Mystery indeed! We continued to stand in the courtyard of the ancient abbey church in the Pyrenean town of Arles sur Tech staring at the marble coffin, grey now with age, which has kept its secret for over a thousand years.

Is it a natural secret or a supernatural one? I have to find out.

I want here, to express my gratitude to the late Canon Barthas, author of the book *"Le Mystère de la Sainte Tombe"* published in 1972, by "Le Meridien" and "La Croix du Midi", without which I could not have discovered this wonder.

7

CHAPTER ONE

THE TOMB'S HISTORY TO AD 1000

In 300 BC the "Via Domitien", the main road connecting Spain and Rome ran past and not far from the little French town of Arles sur Tech which lies close to the Spanish frontier and twenty miles from the Mediterranean Sea. Perhaps Hannibal on his way to fight the Romans in Italy in 217 BC, might even have had a sulphur bath in one of the hot springs which lie three miles, as the crow flies, from this little town.

These baths, like many in this part of the Pyrenees, were already well known in Roman times and one can suppose that the name of the village comes from the Latin word "*Arulae*" referring to the small altars built in those days by grateful people, to thank the various gods for the cures they had received from the waters.

After Hannibal passed by, various barbarian armies fought over this countryside until Charlemagne cleared the area by about AD 800 restoring some sort of peace.

Christianity was already known here by then, but was not very popular with either the Saracen or the Visigoth and as a result many Christian men and women were killed. Some were even buried! In those days coffins were often hewn out of stone and some of these coffins, like the one outside the door of the town church, can still be found elsewhere in the South of France today.

As Charlemagne's peace became established, people began to filter back anew. One such person was a monk called Castellan from a now unknown Benedictine abbey in "The Spanish Lands". In AD 778 he started by setting up "a cell" to which he hoped others, attracted by Saint Benedict's discipline, would come. His choice for the site was close to the hot springs and he used the stones from the ruins of some Gallo-Roman villa which had been ravaged by the Visigoths or perhaps the Saracens who had more recently left the area in the face of Charlemagne's army.

No one knows precisely why, nor exactly when, this religious community moved the three miles from the hot springs to its present location, but it was probably just before AD 900 and the building of this very beautiful XIth century abbey church must have been started here at about that time.

It is thought that the move was authorised by one Suniefred, a member of the powerful "Le Velu" family of Barcelona and we know that this Suniefred was made abbot in AD 881.

Interestingly, when the community moved from the hot springs, the monks brought an old and empty marble coffin with them, which they placed in the forecourt just outside where the main doors of their new church were to be. The new abbey church was first consecrated in AD 1046. A second consecration followed in 1157, after the nave had been reroofed and the ceilings of the side chapels redone in the then new Gothic style.

On the south side of the church, in front of the main doors, is a small courtyard now floored with paving stones. The whole courtyard is surrounded by a very high stone wall.

On your right, as you leave the church by these main doors into the courtyard, is a small enclosure fronted by iron railings. Behind these, in clear view, is the old marble coffin which the monks brought with them and placed there. It still has its heavy marble lid. It rests on two solid stone blocks. It is thus, out in the open, clear of the ground and well away from the walls.

The coffin and its lid are made of white marble having been hewn out of a larger chunk. A white marble quarry existed until quite recently not far from the village. The coffin, after over a thousand years of resting outside the church in the open, now looks a dirty grey to the passer-by and not white at all.

Its exterior measurements can be taken by any enthusiast armed with a tape measure but the internal dimensions were last taken on the 6th March 1950 by a cleaning party, when they took the lid off, cleaned the inside and put the lid back on. The lid hasn't been removed since.

The internal dimensions, taken in 1950 gave the volume as 330.88 dm3 or about 331 litres, thus nearly 73 Imperial Gallons. (See chapter three for details).

On the longer side of the coffin body is a carved logo. A Greek "chi" (X) cut by an "iota" (I). As the perhaps better known "chi" cut by a "rho" (P) meaning "Christos", became more generally used in about the 5th century, this logo must date the coffin from about the 3rd or 4th century. The logo's meaning is either the Greek for "Jesus Christ" or the Greek word "Ichthus", meaning "fish", the symbolic name for the Saviour. It is thus safe to assume that the coffin was intended for a Christian.

Nothing further is known for certain about the coffin, either for whom it was made or indeed if it ever contained a body. What is known, is that the monks around AD 900, treated it with considerable respect, bringing it from the location of the early "cell" near the hot springs, and placing it, empty, outside the entrance to their new church.

In about AD 957, a certain Arnulfe became abbot until his death in about 963. (Precise dates are nowhere recorded in writing). The area, according to some written reports was suffering from plagues and other disasters to such an extent that when his duty required him to go and see the Pope in Rome, Arnulfe decided to request some saint's relics for his abbey. He could then place the abbey and surrounding countryside under the chosen saint's protection.

We would do well to remember here that, as the end of the first millenium approached, not only were people afraid that the end of the world was imminent as could be taken to have been foretold in the Apocalypse but, the vogue in Christian Europe was the collection of the relics of great saints, under whose protection the clergy could and did place people and towns. People were no longer content to just pray to and worship a saint on his feast day in a church dedicated to him, but wished to possess and touch anything which had been his during his life on earth.

Although warnings were put out by bishops to try and prevent gullible people from being defrauded, nevertheless certain clerics extremely well placed, even in Rome itself, but with extremely doubtful moral values, quickly stepped into the growing market. One cleric claiming to have found Moses' rod for parting the waters of the Red Sea, sold it for a fortune! One might also reasonably query how and where one cleric claimed to have found St. John the Baptist's head!

Arnulfe, not wishing to take any risks, put his request to the Pope himself. During the lenten celebrations of about AD 960 Arnulfe, after speaking to the Pope and being granted his request for some relics, sought time for a further night's prayer and reflection before making his decision.

On the following day he asked to be given the relics of Saints Abdon and Sennen, who were very well known at that time. On granting him the relics of these two saints, the Pope ordered that the relics be brought out in a solemn procession and so one can safely assume that we really do have some of their relics here!

Abdon and Sennen were Kurds. Possibly they were princes. They were both officers in King Chahpur's army which, in an effort to forestall a Roman invasion of their land, moved westwards and seized Antioch. Gordian 3 the Roman Emperor (AD 238 — AD 244), reacted swiftly. The Persian army was forced back, Babylon was captured and our two officers as well. Due to their royal status the two prisoners were treated well and seem to have had some considerable freedom of movement for POWs, but this could have been because they would look rather good later in the triumphal processions back in Rome. The invading Roman army had two future emperors among its numbers: Philip the Arabian and Decius. The latter's views on Christians soon became clear and the burial of Christian dead was forbidden.

Abdon and Sennen were witnesses to the killing of Polychronius, The Bishop of Babylon and it was they who buried his body secretly, under the city walls. As the Romans continued their advance, they moved into Cordula the old capital of Kurdistan, the birthplace of the two princes. Despite the Roman's orders, they carried on burying the Christian dead and when caught at the task were flung, in chains, into jail. Later they were taken to Rome.

When Philip the Arabian became emperor after Gordian 3, the two princes were released from prison and lived in Rome. This happy state of affairs was not to last long. Philip's army was defeated by Decius's army at Verona in AD 249 and Decius became emperor. Among the first to die at his hands, or on his orders, was Pope Fabian. Abdon and Sennen did not have to wait very long and, because of their royal rank, they were tried in front of the assembled Senate with Decius presiding. That was on 29th July AD 250.

Having refused, in front of the Senate, to worship the Roman's idols in exchange for their lives and the return of their kingdom, they were condemned to die the following day in the Coliseum. On the morrow, the two young men, after having yet again refused to bow down and worship the Romans' Sun God, were killed by gladiators, tied by the feet and dragged around the arena before being dumped at the foot of the statue of the Sun God outside the Coliseum. The 30th July is thus the Catholic Church's feast day for these two martyrs.

The bodies remained where they had been left for three days until, at great personal risk, Quirinus, a sub deacon, collected the bodies and putting them in a lead coffin, hid them in his house near the Coliseum.

Nineteen years later Quirinus himself was killed but, in AD 312 after the Edict of Milan by Constantine the Great, the bodies of the two martyrs were carried, in perhaps one of the first triumphal processions, to the Pontian Catacomb.

The martyrs' bodies were now placed in an underground room to the right of a sort of niche where a tomb served as an altar. In front of this niche one can still see a square pool dominated by a baptismal font, for the early Christians chose to be baptised close to where those who had died for their faith lay. The water for this pool came and still comes from, an underground spring giving a pure, limpid and ever flowing supply.

The relics of Abdon and Sennen lay in the Pontian Catacomb for several hundred years but, perhaps because they were difficult for pilgrims to approach, or because it was considered wiser to protect them better from the raiding Normans, they were moved.

It is possible that they were moved as early as AD 640 to St. Candide's Church, but certainly during the pontificate of Pope Gregory 4th (827-844) they were moved to St. Mark's Basilica where they still lay when, in about AD 960 the Abbot Arnulfe came to Rome and begged for some relics for his abbey.

Arnulfe was authorised to take, as canon law allowed, half the total quantity of the relics of Saints Abdon and Sennen. Some of their relics are now also to be found in the abbey at Fulda, West Germany and at the Church of St. Medard at Soissons in France.

By canon law, Arnulfe would have had to transport the relics of the two saints in two separate containers in order not to mix them. It is not clear whether he put the relics into two separate barrels or in two halves of one barrel. The artist who did the reredos in the church at Arles sur Tech in 1647, suggests that there were two barrels, but some written reports quote but one barrel, carefully divided.

Arnulfe devised a "cover plan" in the event of interception by pirates or other ill-intentioned people for it should be remembered, that the Moors were still to be found then on the French coast from the Pyrenees to the mouth of the Rhone. He decided to carry wine and water additionally in his barrels so that, a not too detailed search would suggest he was carrying nothing but his journey's drink and certainly not the relics of Christian saints.

Arnulfe embarked at Genoa and landed at Port Illigat, a small sheltered bay two kms from Cadaques on the Costa Brava where a small chapel reminds us of his arrival.

After a difficult journey, Arnulfe arrived in Arles sur Tech on the 24th October, a date celebrated in the area. The stories handed down by local tradition are fascinating but now of course impossible to check: Celestial beings who steered the ship through a terrible Mediterranean storm, church bells ringing without the bell-ringers being present etc. as Arnulfe and his small train passed by. The "train" in fact went via La Junquera and then the Monastery of Saint Mary of Panissars which was a dependence of the abbey at Arles sur Tech.

Arnulfe's actions on arrival at Arles suggest that he may have drawn water for his barrels from the pool at the Pontian Catacomb where the saints' bodies had rested for so long, for he did not just throw the water away but poured it and the relics into the empty coffin. Later he extracted the bulk of the relics to put them into two more suitable reliquaries, leaving behind in the coffin, only those bones which are still there today.

In each of the two centre pillars supporting the roof of the church, the builders left a chamber which could have been used for relics and other precious objects. It is probable that the reliquaries for Saints Abdon and Sennen were sheltered in these lockable chambers until a more suitable place could be found. The present-day two silver reliquaries were available only by 1440, and the side altar with its special reredos was completed by Lazare Tramulles of Perpignan only in 1647.

CHAPTER TWO

STORY OF THE MONKS FROM AD **1000**
UNTIL THE FRENCH REVOLUTION

We can find very little in the way of the history of this monastery collected in one place. The French Revolution did not help for the two or three remaining monks in about 1793 fled with their abbot to Italy where the abbot died as did probably his companions. One hears no more of the religious community in Arles sur Tech and the church became a parish church.

The church building itself, was desecrated by the "Louts" and the abbey records probably fared no better.

One can learn a bit from other sources and I have summarised some of these to round off the picture of the Abbey of "Sainte Marie".

1178
The King of Majorca forbade the construction of any other castle or fortification near the abbey. This indicates that the abbey itself was protected not only by the king, but by solid walls as well.

1211
One can read of the donation to the abbey by William Gaucelme of 100 sous, a small fortune in those days.

1235
The population of Arles rose in revolt against Abbot Arnaud Berenguer, who was both the spiritual head of the monastery and the secular head of the town. This sort of revolt was not unknown at that time in Europe but not many of the subsequent agreements can still be found in county archives. The "Peasants Revolt" in England in 1381, against King Richard II is better documented!

The Bishop of Elne with a certain Mr Goterdies, an early example of "Arbitrators" for disputes, intervened and brought peace back again. Among the six points of their charter we can read that the villagers

15

could again have their corn ground by the abbey mills "at a just price" and would not have to pay "more than one loaf in twenty-five for the use of the abbey ovens". History doesn't relate what the abbot charged before but it must have been quite a bit more to have caused the riot!

1350
Berenger de Perapertusa was abbot until 1361 when he was "posted" to Nicosia in Cyprus where he became bishop in 1379. While in post there he probably met a certain Jean de Pobol who in 1401 was made a canon and the doyen of Nicosia.

It was this Jean who founded the clerical benefice in the Convent of the Holy Saviour in Perpignan. The requirement for the priest in this convent entirely of nuns was that he should be old and impotent (*"Sit homo senex et indebilis ad sobolem procreandam"*) and added that one must not tempt providence!

1364
We learn that Pierre Roger de Beaufort was abbot until approximately 1368. His life history is interesting for he was made a cardinal at the age of seventeen, in 1338 by his uncle, Pope Clement VI. (Was abbot then demotion?!) In December 1370 he left the abbey to become Pope Gregory XI, at the age of forty-two. It was he who replaced the papacy in Rome after its lengthy stay in Avignon. He was the last French pope.

1394
The "Guild of the Saints' Bodies" was founded after twenty-two sous had been left in a will by a certain Thomas del Mollo who was a merchant in Prats de Mollo, a village some fifteen miles further up the valley from Arles and used by the kings of Majorca as a summer residence.

1425
The guild had probably by now collected enough money and so ordered a first silver bust for Saint Abdon's relics.

1440
The guild ordered a second and similar bust for Saint Sennen's relics. The two busts were made by the Perpignan silversmith Michael Alerigues.

1612
This is the first recorded occasion when the relics of Saints Abdon and Sennen travelled in their silver reliquaries for three days, with an escort

from the town to Perpignan. It is recorded that after a solemn procession around the town the rains came, putting an end to the drought which had been the reason for the request for the visit. A second similar visit was requested and made in 1691 for the same reason and with the same result!

1647
The Perpignan sculptor Lazare Tramulles completed the reredos for the chapel of Saints Abdon and Sennen. The following table shows this reredos:

Crucifixion				
Flagellation of the Saints	The Saints in front of the Sun God	Immaculate Conception	Beheading the Saints	The Lions and the Saints
Exhumation in Rome	A miracle with the wine	Saints Abdon and Sennen	The Mule at Arles	The Relics in the Reliquaries
Saints refuse to worship Idols	Saints refuse Harlots in Prison	Coat of Arms of the Saints	Trial of Saints	Condemnation of Saints

1738
Another visit was made with the relics but this time to Ceret as the people of that town wished to show their personal devotion to the saints.

1792
We come now to the French Revolution. The law of 10 September was passed forbidding the veneration of superstitious objects and requiring their surrender (if they were valuable) to the national authorities.

B

1793

Into the arena now quietly stepped Joseph Mas of Arles, better known as Turrie, he whisked the busts away and hid them first, in the "Cortal d'En Rigall" (The sheep prairie at Rigall) which is five twisty miles from Arles and 1,600 feet higher up. Then, for fear of further betrayal, in a cave hidden in the forest in the mountains and as the record reports, "known only to Turrie".

The town council next reported to Perpignan, the extraordinary theft of the silver busts!

7 February 1793

The monks having fled, the town council was officially in charge of the abbey and they had not handed over the silver busts. Such disobedience was not to be tolerated and a sharp letter came from the county town of Perpignan.

The town council was advised that the National Assembly was to be informed if, within three days, the busts were not handed in or in their place, an equivalent quantity of silver to the value of the busts, which was estimated by the Perpignan silversmiths at 1,000 ecus. The town was advised that failure to comply would result in a sufficiently numerous body of troops being sent for as long as was necessary to arrange compliance with these orders and at the expense of the town!! The arrival of the Louts and the desecration is covered in chapter three.

CHAPTER THREE

TOMB'S HISTORY FROM AD 1000 TO 1964

About AD 1200
It is not known with any certainty when water was first drawn from the tomb nor when the first person was healed but we do have an interesting record of a very ancient healing which dates from the last years of the 12th century and no visitor to the Holy Tomb can avoid seeing it.

Fixed onto the wall of the small courtyard and dominating the sarcophagus, one sees a high relief in marble, representing a life-sized person, arms crossed on his chest. The style is that of the recumbant figures often found on ancient funeral monuments. (See pages 34 & 35.)

In place of a nose, one sees a hole in the middle of his face. Above the head one reads a small inscription from which we learn that Squire Gaucelme of Telet died in 12 . . (the figures for the tens and units have disappeared). The local archives however record the name of this squire who in his will dated 1211, asked to be buried in the monastery where he had been cured and to which he made a very generous gift. A phenomenon such as this tomb could not pass unnoticed and the first official enquiry was made in 1529:

21 January 1529
It was during a war between the French and the Spanish. A detachment of the Spanish army passed through Arles and the officers and the men visited the Holy Tomb. During the many days they stayed in the town, they drew off as much water as they needed from this tomb and many felt themselves cured of various illnesses. Additionally, at the moment of leaving, each soldier took with him as much water as he could carry.

The official enquiry recorded that the volume of water drawn off was three times the volume that the sarcophagus could contain and which anyhow, was as full after the departure of the troops as it had been before their arrival!

This authentic report carries the signatures of a number of witnesses, among others that of John Guardia, Rector of the Parish Church of Saint-Sauveur, the abbey's rival!

1587
A second enquiry was made in 1587. An apostolic visitor wished to satisfy himself that there hadn't been any mistake due to natural causes. To this end he summoned the senior officials and the more important inhabitants of the town to conduct an examination in their presence. It was verified by all the witnesses "that the sarcophagus had no opening in its lower part and that the small columns which support it were perfectly solid and with no cracks through which water, even if there were a spring under the flagstones, could penetrate into the coffin body". All the witnesses signed.

23 March 1752
Yet another enquiry was made on 23 March 1752 by the officials of the Town Hall, several burgesses and other honourable citizens of the town. They ordered that the sarcophagus be taken away from its ordinary resting-place where it is supported on the two movable marble stones, to see if there were some duct or other conduit which could introduce any extraneous water into the Holy Tomb. After having seen and examined in the presence of all the people there assembled, they declared "that it was by nature impossible that any alien water could communicate in the Holy Tomb". All the witnesses again signed.

November 1825
For the inhabitants of Arles, the crucial event, among those which history has recorded, is that of a second "birth" of the water in the Holy Tomb in 1795 when the witnesses saw the physical verification of the words of the psalm: *"Eduxit aquam de petra"*: "The Lord brought water out from stone."

The event is reported for us in an official document covering the proceedings of 29 and 30 November 1825 when the parish priest, ten women and thirteen men were heard as witnesses.

They were questioned in the church itself, in front of a large gathering, including the mayor, his assistant, a justice of the peace, the registrar, two solicitors, six members of the town council, two churchwardens, twenty other witnesses and "other most notable persons of the town".

From all the evidence, all basically the same, and which it would be idle to quote in its entirety, we have made the following synthesis for the reader.

REPORT
"After having taken the oath, the twenty-four witnesses each in turn and separately related their memories of this event, these were immediately taken down in writing."

"In the month of May 1794, a detachment of troops, known as the "louts" (Allobroges), being part of the Republican army on its way to Spain, stopped off at Arles. After having sacked the church and burnt a number of objects of veneration, these fanatics tore off the cover of the sarcophagus, overturned the coffin from its double socle and put in filth.

"It stayed in this state for sixteen months without anyone daring either to right it or to clean it. However some of the relics which it enclosed were able to be saved thanks to the presence of mind and the devotion of some pious people.

"The Holy Tomb conserved for some time a little water in amongst the filth and dust which the wind stacked up in it.

"In the month of October 1795, it at last became possible to celebrate the Catholic religion in the church again. A priest, the Reverend Michel Bosch, had already been back in Arles for more than a year and several people beseeched him with persistence, to right the tomb. He acceded to their requests.

"A group of people assembled at the venerable monument; the coffin was completely dry, but stained by a lot of filth. Cauldrons of hot water were brought and the inside of the tomb was washed three times. Then it was rinsed with fresh water several times.

"Some women left to get clean cloths to dry it. They returned with these and at once set to work. To the great surprise of these women and of all those people present, one saw that as the women rubbed with the cloths, the water reappeared instantly on the inner side of the said tomb, ran down and collected at the bottom, which made the women stop drying and their cloths remained wet.

"One of the helpers couldn't restrain his emotions and cried out 'It's a miracle!' The word flew from mouth to mouth among the numerous spectators, and the majority cried tears of joy seeing that the Lord was recompensing their faith by permitting, in their presence, the renewal of the miracle of the water.

"One woman, Marguerite Berdaguer, had replaced in the tomb the portion of the relics which it had been possible to save at the time of the desecration, and the Reverend Bosch demanded that the cover be put back on the coffin. Next the assembly withdrew much affected.

"Three hours later, some people returned to the scene, curious to see whether the water had risen. Mr Valent Commails, house owner, inserted a straw into the tomb to measure the depth of water; it was of the thickness of a finger (10 to 12 mm).

"On the following day, the same Mr Commails returned with the Reverend Bosch; they found that the water, having risen, now measured about an inch (28 mm)."

Some days later, it was the feast of "la Vinguda dels Sants" ("The Arrival of the Saints": 24 October). On the Sunday following, the day of the solemnity, the Reverend Bosch, before the Mass, went in procession to the tomb, had the lid taken off and it was noted that there was then a depth of about a "pan" (25 cms). There was now drawn off a bottle for a parishioner of Fourques who had asked for it.

Next the Reverend Bosch had the lid sealed with iron crampons, which remained in place until the cleaning in 1950.

Following this, the priest distributed this same water to all of the faithful who asked for some and who turned up in a crowd. He testified that he had distributed at least 150 bottles during one single morning of the Patron Saints' Feast without having noticed the slightest fall in the level of the water.

1848
The Reverend Juval, (parish priest from 1843 to 1883) realised in 1848 that water was gradually being lost through a small crack in the lower part of the tomb. He had the tomb hoisted to a height of seventy-five centimetres and during the repairs everyone could see that the supporting stone blocks showed no sign of interior ducts, which fact he brought especially to the attention of his parishioners.

1936
A Parisian chemist, Monsieur Oliviero, claimed to have analysed the water from the Holy Tomb and said that he had found it to have the same chemical composition as that of a fountain not far from the Cloisters and supplied with town water.

Based on this, Mr Oliviero formulated all manner of hypotheses to explain the arrival of the water right into the sarcophagus. The newspaper *"Journal des Débats"* printed these "revelations", which concluded with a negation of a miracle. The Parisian article was reproduced in the newspaper *"L'Indépendant"* of Perpignan.

1936 to 1947
The Reverend Maler who was parish priest from 1936 to 1947, also had the tomb water analysed by a chemist from the north of France who reported that he found it chemically pure like distilled water, with only some traces of chalk, explainable by its contact with the marble of the

tomb. i.e.— Nothing like town water!

In March 1941 when he had the sarcophagus lifted twice by pilgrims, each time in front of more than 200 people, he declared: "I do not believe that one can explain the origin of this water logically".

3 April 1942

A report was made by some of the town officials and is given in full, as the families of those concerned are still living here:

"Messrs Maurice Vuillemin, Pierre Sala, Prospere Dunyach, Jacques Galangau, Henri Galangau, Joseph Comes, Jean Cordimi, Sans, François Oms, François Pujade.

"We report, on looking through a hole in the gap, that the sarcophagus is completely full, the water is flush with the edge and the liquid even overflows. A drop falls from time to time.

"The parish priest informs us that he has drawn off water recently; it has not rained since and the water again fills the sarcophagus. Thus it hasn't rained for some days and the water continues to drip over the edge.

"We place a plate at the point where the drops fall to the ground."

The Parish Report of 23 June 1942

"We have been suffering from a period of intense drought for two months. On two or three occasions it has scarcely rained even lightly. We measure the water-level. The sarcophagus is nearly full; the level lacks barely three centimetres to overflowing."

Signatures of the Revd Maler — Parish Priest; Messrs François Oms, François Pujade.

1950

The official report of the cleaning and the resurgence of the water:

"The sixth of March one thousand nine hundred and fifty (holy year), from 1730 hours to 1900 hours, was carried out the opening of the Holy Tomb. This operation had been decided upon in order to carry out a complete cleansing of the inside of the sarcophagus. It will be seen later that this operation had become necessary as a considerable deposit of mud had formed at the bottom of the stone coffin, coming from the dust which the wind had blown into the interior through the small gaps between the body and the cover. The volume of the muddy deposit which one extracted, leaves one to suppose that the opening of the Holy Tomb hadn't been done for a very long time. Assisting at this operation:

The Reverend Dalqué — Parish Priest,

Mr François Pujade — Wholesaler. Secretary of the Town Information Office,

24

Mr Jacques Sola — Farrier,
Mr Prosper Dunyach — Master-Mason,
Miss Joséphine Musquière.

"Mr Dunyach proceeded first to remove the fastening cramps which hold the cover on the body of the sarcophagus. This done, thanks to some pincers, the heavy marble cover was lifted and wedged with planks, then moved to one side by means of sliding it along the planks and supports. The interior was thus offered to the sight of the five witnesses. A strong odour of mustiness came out. The bottom of the sarcophagus was hidden under a layer of black mud, hardly damp and several centimetres thick. The Holy Tomb was completely dry: no layer of water was found in the sarcophagus. One could see clearly the place (which formed a clean area in the middle of the mud) where the end of the siphon scraped the bottom of the sarcophagus when one siphoned up the water. The layer of mud was split, cracked. A piece of copper pipe coming from a siphon which had been inadvertently let fall, was found mixed up with the mud. Although of copper and although it had lain for a very great number of years in the coffin, this piping carried no trace of verdigris.

"Mixed up with the slime, we recovered a portion of small bones of which the dimensions ran from some millimetres to five or six centimetres. There were it seems some particles of skull bones and without doubt, a metatarsus. These relics are those of the holy martyrs Abdon and Sennen which the Abbot Arnulfe brought from Rome about a thousand years ago and of which a small quantity was placed in the Holy Tomb. But these bones belong to the aforementioned two martyrs who perished in 251, thus 1700 years ago. We piously sorted and extracted from the mud all these bits of bone which, even after seventeen centuries, have kept the hardness of ordinary bone. The metatarsus in particular has suffered no alteration. Yet these relics have remained in the tomb, sometimes in water, sometimes in free air.

"We proceeded to scrape out the mud which filled a large box and whose weight can be evaluated at two kilos. We vigorously brushed the sides and the bottom using a scrubbing brush and a metal brush. As the stone is not smooth but pitted with holes from the chisel which made it, the work of cleaning it took quite long. When practically all the mud had been removed, we proceeded to rinse the sides and the bottom using water squeezed out of a sponge. We also carefully cleaned the horizontal edges and the four lateral surfaces with a vigorous brushing. The clean stone indicated clearly that the sarcophagus is of white marble.

"At the bottom, over a length of some fifty centimetres, we noticed a superficial crack in the stone. Obviously, we did justice to the slanderous rumour which claimed that there was a duct ending at the stone coffin. There does not exist the smallest hole. The lid is perfectly clean and dry on the underside at the hollowed out part. The marble is a yellowish white. The stone is very clean and we did not detect the slightest condensation. The bottom is not lying absolutely horizontally: the sarcophagus has been laid in such a way that the waters collect in the little hollow where the end of the siphon reaches. It is thus slightly raised on the side nearest the church.

"Mr Dunyach carefully took the internal measurements of the sarcophagus which are the following: length 1.76 m; width 0.47 m; depth 0.40 m. The sides fall vertically, one can thus know exactly the capacity of the Holy Tomb; the calculation gives 176 ★ 47 ★ 40 = 330.88 dm3. Consequently, the volume of the sarcophagus is thus to within a few centilitres, 331 litres.

"We are thus a long way from the figures which have been put forward in different tomes and the capacity is far superior to that which one supposed. We are not giving the exterior dimensions, which anyone can measure easily. However remember that the thickness of the sides varies from eighty to ninety-five millimetres.

"When the work of cleaning of which we have spoken above had been finished, we carefully dried the interior with a clean cloth. (The miracle of October 1795 — oozing from the sides — did not recur). There is reason to believe that the Holy Tomb had not been opened since that date, that is to say for 155 years. We washed the holy relics in water and Mr Pujade again replaced them in the Holy Tomb, at the end nearest the church.

"The cover was put back in place, while awaiting the repositioning of the sealing cramps and the running of some cement into the gap around the circumference.

"All the undersigned witnesses, present during the operation, attest to the exactitude of the terms of this official report and sign."

F. Dalqué. Prosper Dunyach. F. Pujade. J. Sala. J. Musquière.

12 April 1951
Newspaper report (just over a year later): To the above so detailed report, we must add a *post-scriptum* from the Perpignan newspaper *"L'Indépendant"* of 12 April 1951, reporting the return of the water in the mysterious coffin.

After reproducing the above document in *toto*, the newspaper continued:

"Let us add that eight days after this cleaning operation, the water appeared again in the sarcophagus. Actually, the depth is about twenty centimetres; which indicates a volume of water of 165 litres, or more than half the total capacity".

1964

Distribution of the water on the day of the annual fête on 30 July 1964. (Report by the late Revd Canon Barthas of Toulouse.)

"On the eve, I went to the presbytery to alert the senior priest of my wish to verify closely what the effect of the annual distribution was on the internal volume of the water. I asked him to be good enough on the 30th morning, to measure the level of the water before the distribution and then again in the evening when the general distribution was finished. He told me that as soon as he got up, he would be mobbed by pilgrims and wouldn't be free before midday. This was why he was happy to come with me that evening at 7 p.m., to measure the water-level. The millimetre ruler registered twenty-seven centimetres; we didn't think of noting whether it was a few millimetres more or less. Was it necessary? Even if one only drew off twenty litres, the difference would be sufficiently noticeable in centimetres because each centimetre corresponds to a difference of 8.272 litres (length 176 cm $\star$ width 47 cm = 8.272).

"On the 30th, from 6 a.m., pilgrims filled the small courtyard which fronts the church; the parish priest celebrated a first Mass and was then retained in the sacristy until a second Mass at 8 a.m. At 9.30 a.m., the procession called the "Rodella of Montbolo" took place; it was the 499th time that the clergy and faithful of Arles, carrying solemnly the two reliquary busts of the two martyred saints, went to greet, at the entry to the town, the annual gift of the neighbouring parish. As a result of a vow made in 1465, the Parish of Montbolo presents to the martyred saints a sort of crown made of a long rolled up ribbon of liturgical candle wax (Rodella). On returning to the church, Mass was sung by Canon Coll, the Parish Priest of Amélie les Bains.

"After the service, the distribution of the water began. A young neighbourhood priest, born in the parish, was given this task. He drew off the water using the little metal siphon/pump. He allowed me to help him count the bottles which he filled without stopping. The press of the crowd prevented us from counting with meticulous precision. Many applicants had no receptacle and so presented the twenty-five centilitre bottle sold for 1.20 francs by a vestry nun. Some minutes after midday, no further "clients" presented themselves. We accounted for 100 bottles, but there had been a variety of other receptacles, tins and bottles, whose total volume we estimated as a minimum of ten litres.

"After the evening service, a further distribution was made; the same priest in charge. An elderly Arlesian remarked to me that, in the old days the priest for this service, wore a surplice and stole. I told him that I had seen the young priest make a pious sign of the cross before beginning.

"We counted thirty-five standard bottles and also some other containers and other bottles. However the senior parish priest came and filled two one litre bottles, because it is necessary for him to have a small reserve of the water to satisfy callers who ask for some at odd moments.

"When the gate of the little enclosure had been shut, some other people turned up whom we directed to the presbytery. Then we finalised the day's calculations: thirty-five litres in the morning, twelve in the afternoon. Total forty-seven.

"We would have liked at this moment to have measured the water-level, but it was impossible to get hold of the parish priest. However with his agreement, we went and invited Mr François Pujade, the president and some members of the town Information Office.

"They came and there was also a photographer present, a visiting priest and a pilgrim. The millimetre ruler recorded 26.7 cms. Thus at the very outside two or three millimetres less than that on the eve, where we hadn't bothered to check the millimetres. One can thus say that in spite of having drawn off nigh on half a hecto-litre of water, the level hadn't varied, while naturally it should have sunk by about six centimetres.

"After the first measurement, not a single drop of rain had fallen; besides, the whole month had been very dry, apart from the hail storms of the 24th and 25th."

Well so much for the men of faith. But what about the rest of us? You perhaps, or me?

CHAPTER FOUR

OVER SIMPLIFIED SOLUTIONS

The 20th century, having seen the development of the natural sciences, has given birth in many minds to an absolute confidence in the power of human reasoning. The laws of nature are unalterable, therefore there is no miracle for which science can not sooner or later find a natural explanation. This certainty has led to the following simplistic solutions being put forward and it will be sensible to shoot these down straight away so that they are not boringly resurrected:

Fraud; some secret piping; the filling of the tomb by rain-water or the condensation of humid air; even the porousness of marble!

1. Fraud

Let's start with this, the most ridiculous of all: it is the clergy or sacristans themselves who put the water in the tomb.

On giving the matter the slightest thought, there must have been, constantly over the last ten centuries, a sort of protector of frauds such that no inhabitant of Arles or elsewhere, has ever caught a prior, a monk, a priest, a vicar or indeed anybody else in the act of fraudulently putting water into the tomb which is in the open and outside the church.

This sort of solution also ignores the fact that scientists from three different countries have proved that the tomb water is unlike ANY local water. So where would these nocturnal fillers have got it from?!

2. Secret piping

The sceptics next move to the theory of a secret pipe which feeds water into the sarcophagus from a reservoir or an unknown spring.

Over the past centuries, this notion has attracted the attention of many people because it was the motivation behind some searching enquiries. Let's remember however that the sarcophagus is well away from the walls; one can walk a full circle round it and examine all its sides. It is absolutely unattached. Two marble blocks support it and they themselves are just placed on the stone floor. Two men can easily lift the tomb by one end to separate it from its base and can then repeat the experiment at the other end. The casual visitor however should not attempt this as tinkering with the tomb, without permission, is likely to result in the arrival of the gendarmerie and your French then had better be very good!

The Revd Maler (Parish Priest from 1936 to 1947), had the sarcophagus lifted on two occasions, as mentioned in chapter three, each time in front of more than two hundred people and then drew all the spectators' attention to the supporting blocks and the ground on which they stood which had no pipes nor other means of resupply.

If the resupply of water were furnished by such a method, it would be just as fraudulent as direct filling and, during ten centuries, it is impossible that it would not have been discovered.

3. Rain-water

If the water doesn't come from below, then it must come from above. It must be rain-water which, falling on the surface of the cover manages, by one means or another, to penetrate into the tomb. Why it doesn't also go out of the bottom, sometimes causes a little difficulty, yet this explanation was put forward most succinctly in a report contained in the local newspaper *"L'Indépendant des Pyrénées Orientales"* on the 26 May 1936 and signed under the pseudonym of "Ittey".

The article referred back to an article which had appeared ten years previously in a paper called *"Journal des Débats"* written by a certain Mr Oliviero, of whom we have also spoken in chapter three. Having recalled the points of the controversy raised in the previously mentioned article, Mr Ittey claims to put an end to the affair by giving us his personal point of view. For him:

". . . the content of the sarcophagus is common or garden rain-water collected in lesser or greater abundance depending on the intensity of the rainfall, thanks to the non adhesion of the cover to the lower part of the sarcophagus. This, on the side facing the wall and so therefore invisible to the public who are not able to enter the locked but not covered enclosure where the sarcophagus is placed, presents additionally this peculiarity that the outer edge of the cover lies well inside the line of the outer edge of the body of the tomb; this singularly facilitates the penetration of water into the interior."

The said gentleman hardly knows what he is talking about, for if the sarcophagus is really in contact with the wall, how is it possible for people to walk all round it? Over the centuries remember, thousands of people have passed by there!

Mr Ittey gives us another proof of his ingenious theory. He speaks of a priest from Amélie les Bains (the nearest village) and whose name he doesn't give, who had, after successive experiments, proved that the tomb, emptied of its contents, remained empty as long as no rain fell.

"On the other hand," apparently said this unknown cleric, "it had been possible, after showers, to draw off from the sarcophagus a number of bottles in proportion to the intensity of these showers; fine and continuous rain gave a larger volume than hard storms."

It is perfectly true that, on the side facing the wall, the outer edge of the cover doesn't, by a few millimetres, correspond with the outer edge of the coffin body, but it means that an adventurous drop has still to penetrate between the two full thickness of the marble, eight or more centimetres, to arrive inside, which certainly limits the number of drops that make it.

In 1936, the Revd Maler made some precise observations during a rainy spell with the help of a doctor and a chemist from Perpignan. In fact they saw only a few drops introduce themselves into the gap between the cover and the body. This is the phenomenon known by the name of capillary attraction which causes a liquid which is poured slowly, to run along the body of the recipient rather than to fall straight down.

But how could the few drops so fortuitously introduced change their chemical analysis and supply the 50 to 100 bottles drawn off on average on the 30th July alone?

4. The porousness of marble

The imagination of the rationalist resorts now to yet another explanation:

The stone of the sarcophagus allows water to pass through it, it is porous.

It is not thought that the textbooks of physics or geology generally classify marble as a porous rock, that is to say one which absorbs the water coming into contact with it or the humidity in the air which surrounds it.

Additionally, in our atmosphere, any body sufficiently porous to allow water to pass into it is equally able to let water pass out of it, the atmospheric pressure being the same on both sides.

It is not unreasonable to conclude that if rain-water can get in, then the same rain-water will get out!

CHAPTER FIVE

VARIOUS MODERN SCIENTIFIC THEORIES

Certain modern scholars look for other causes. In essence, they all come back to one single principle: condensation of the humidity in the atmosphere helped by temperature differences. One might call this theory: water generation by "atmospheric captors". Almost all refer to the little gap which separates the cover from the body of the coffin over nearly its whole length.

In theory, it is not impossible that on one or another part of the globe's surface a spring can be formed by the phenomenon of condensation, for example in very permeable ground, such as a desert or in dunes, sited on top of an impermeable strata.

Although one doesn't see how the Holy Tomb can be compared with a sandy or fissured soil, several scientific reviews have wished to show that the water which is drawn off can have no other origin.

On the 1st of March 1933, the review *"La Nature"* published a study by a Mr Paul Basiaux on "Atmospheric Captors" of the air's humidity. He stated that ". . . for centuries a captor has been functioning in the county of the Eastern Pyrenees . . . the joints are not absolutely smooth, which allows the humidity to penetrate freely. This water whose mysterious resupply has, on more than one occasion, made people believe in a fraud, is considered locally to be miraculous."

He concluded: "In fact, we are in the presence of an "Atmospheric Well", of a captor of the humidity in the atmosphere."

However he didn't study the question too carefully as he stated this capturing explained how "one may draw off from the sarcophagus in good or bad years one hundred litres of water".

As the figure is nearly 600 litres one must conclude that Mr Paul Basiaux's "atmosperic well" is not the whole answer!

The following year in the review *"Savoir"* (the January issue), Mr Henri de Varigny again took up the study of "Wells in the atmosphere". He wrote at length of those in Bizerte (Tunisia). "They are sand dunes

31

MAP 1

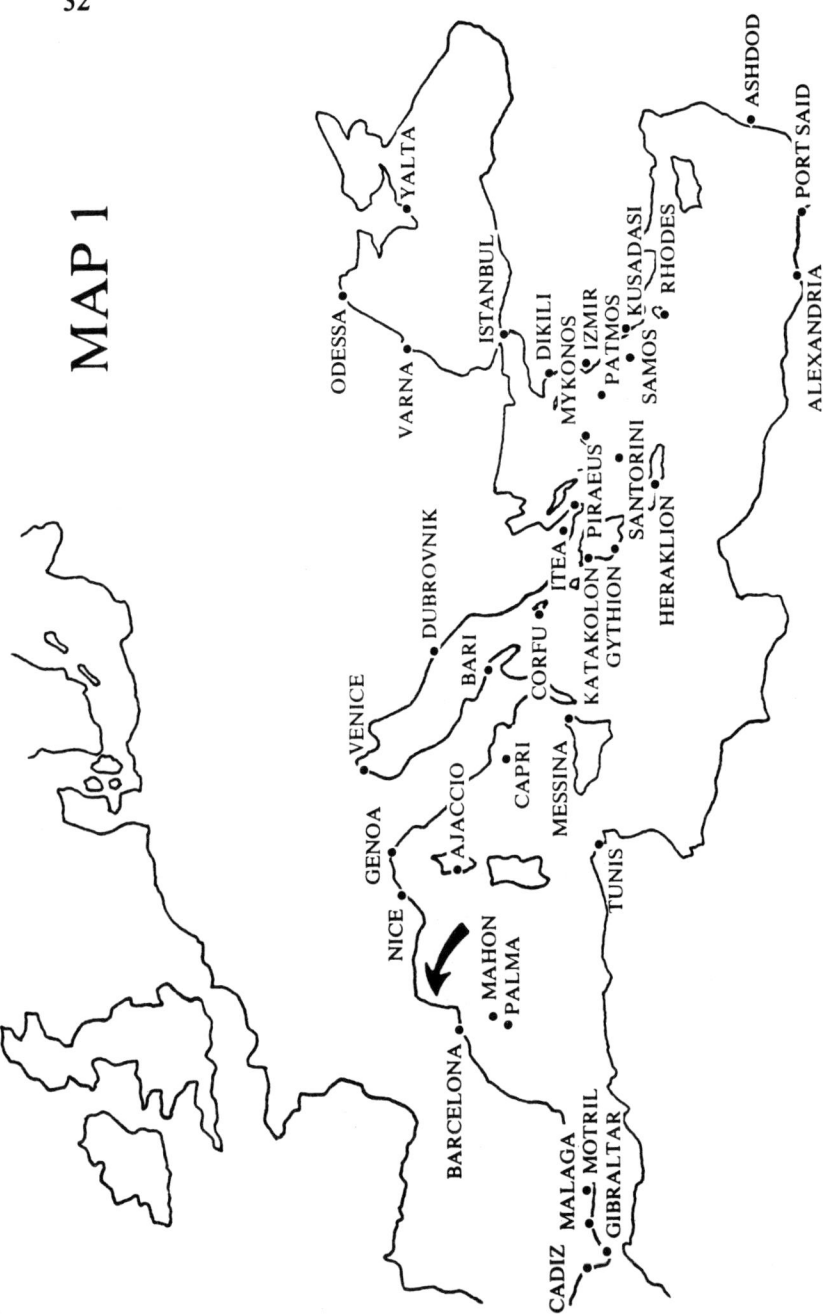

View looking West of Courtyard and Main Church Door

Closer view of Coffin

Close up of Ex-voto

Close up of Coffin looking West

Close up of Coffin looking North

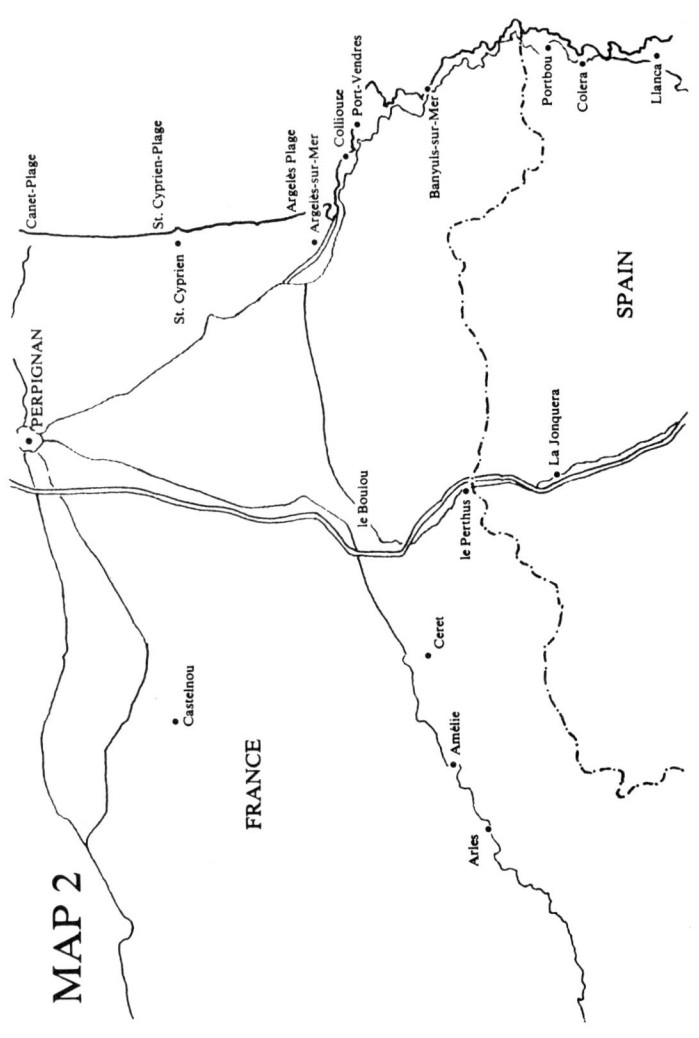

MAP 2

FRANCE

SPAIN

PERPIGNAN

Canet-Plage

St. Cyprien-Plage

St. Cyprien

Argelès Plage
Argelès-sur-Mer
Collioure
Port-Vendres
Banyuls-sur-Mer

Portbou
Colera
Llança

le Boulou

le Perthus

La Jonquera

Ceret

Castelnou

Amélie

Arles

which serve as condensers where the springs rise which are in part captured to supply the town." Putting the sarcophagus of Arles into the same category as the dunes, he concluded: "The phenomenon considered is well explained by science."

There are however here two huge problems. Firstly, it is very difficult to put an accumulation of grains of sand into the same category as a coffin hewn out of solid marble; and secondly, enquiries made among several repatriated Tunisians who had lived in Bizerte did not reassure one of the facts of which Mr de Varigny spoke. Many of them had never heard of them!

In order to be sure however, the Reverend Canon R. Cassou, who had been the senior priest of Bizerte for thirteen years, and who had never heard tell of these dunes either, wrote to an Arab friend "a Civil Servant with the Public Works Department".

His reply was that:

"The town of Bizerte is supplied from two principal natural springs, Ain-Damouss and Ain-Bourass. Both tapped supplies are gravity fed. In the past, two other springs: Ain-Berda and Ain-Ghezala, were also used. At the present time, they are dried up; one has supplemented them from pumping stations in the region to the north and from the region to the south. This gives Bizerte a considerable advantage compared with other Tunisian towns, it is the one supplied by natural water, the others drawing their water from the wadis or dams."

There doesn't appear to be any doubt, Mr de Varigny was very badly briefed indeed!

Mr René Colas, Director of the French Association for the Study of Water, (Association Française pour l'Etude des Eaux), gave a conference in February 1957, in Geneva, which was reported in a magazine called *"Bulletin de l'Association des anciens élèves de l'école de chimie de Paris"*. He dealt with the question of the sarcophagus without bringing forward any new elements to solve the ancient phenomenon.

For him, the origin of this water in the coffin can be explained by:

"This collection of sufficiently favourable circumstances: Northern exposition in a deep courtyard where the sun does not penetrate, the surrounding architectural ensemble, comprising massive constructions probably forming a thermal force, and especially a good circulation of warm and humid air pouring over the southern wall, cooling at ground level, whose humidity condenses in the body of the sarcophagus."

All these factors might favour humidity but not to the extent that a visitor is struck by it or that one can account for the origin of the contents of the coffin from it. Mr Colas's conclusions were however less categorical than those of Mr de Varigny. Mr Colas said:

"We put forward these thoughts and these notes for what they are worth, as precise measurements have not been taken around this very singular sarcophagus. What is certain, is that the parish priest can, during each summer month, distribute up to 100 litres of miraculous water and that one has seen, at certain times, the sarcophagus overflow. The condensations called "occult" and much disputed, haven't entirely given up their secret. Under these circumstances the 'mystery' remains complete."

The magazine *"Geographia"* also interested itself with the Holy Tomb in January 1958. Mr Paul Basiaux's theory of the atmospheric wells was resurrected. A certain Mr P. Fortunat, an engineer with the P.T.E. in Algeria reports three such wells able to compete with that of Arles. One at Theodosia, one at Bizerte and that at Bel-Air near Montpellier. He owned to being very poorly briefed on Theodosia (in the Crimea).

In fact the condenser apparatus which one uses there, was the subject of a communication from Mr Hitier of the Agricultural Academy in 1925:

"On the heights dominating the town of Theodosia itself, one can see the man-made pile of limestone rocks, measuring some thirty metres long by twenty-five metres wide and ten metres high. They were broken down into thirteen large divisions and connected by stone pipes to 114 cisterns which would have furnished the town with drinking water.

"Unfortunately these installations haven't worked for centuries and we remain ignorant about many of the things which are involved with them. Above all, we do not know if these captors whose total volume must be close to 100,000 cubic metres, were not in fact a kind of reservoir retaining rain-water and keeping it cool."

One can see no possible comparison between these enormous sorts of sumps, full of broken stones, and the presumed captor of our sarcophagus, a monolithic coffin protected from the rain by a cover. A Russian engineer, Zibold, tried to put the Theodosia system back into working order, but his work was destroyed during the 1914-1918 war.

At the physics and climatology establishment of the Agricultural Institute at Bel-Air (Montpellier), they tried to imitate, on a smaller scale, the sumps of Theodosia because the climate of the Mediterranean Languedoc has a certain analogy with that of the Crimea. Although Professor Chaptal was not the first "inventor" of the atmospheric captor, it has been named after him.

They constructed in the open air, with no shelter, a kind of resevoir having a three metre square base and a height of 2.50 metres which was filled with limestone rocks. The results were positive but insufficient to extend the project. It was noted that the hottest days supplied the most water. During the six hottest months (April to September) in 1930, it produced a little more than eighty-seven litres and, during the same period the following year when the conditions were less favourable, a little more than forty litres.

It must be clear that there is no comparison possible between a captor able to hold twenty-three cubic metres and our sarcophagus which is more than sixty times smaller and which moreover, isn't filled with limestone rocks. In spite of this it supplies to those who ask a considerably greater volume of water and is considered to be totally indifferent to changes of temperature.

The radiesthesist's solution.
In 1954, a certain Mr Baradat, retired professor of the Casablanca Lycée and Director of the *"Review of the Radiesthesist"* having read about the tomb at Arles came on a Sunday evening in August in the hope that the movements of his pendulum would guide him to the source of the tomb's water.

On the Monday he spent four hours working with his pendulum around the tomb and the sanctuary. On the following day the local newspaper *L'Indépendant"* published a note inviting the public to assemble on that same day in front of the church to hear the professor speak.

About 200 people attended and he renewed his experiments for them with the pendulum. It was noted that the pendulum moved excitedly at one point on the lid, one point on the side and at one point on the bottom of the tomb. These points he called "humid" points.

At ground level under the tomb and at ground level all over the enclosure paved with stone, where the tomb lies, the pendulum remained inert. He said this was the most important finding.

Under the chapel beside the tomb's enclosure, the pendulum discovered a strong current which had no common identity with the town water.

The parish priest presented Mr Baradat with two containers, one containing tomb water and the other town water. Mr Baradat's diagnosis was that the town water was NNE (North, North, East) thus according to him, ferruginous and slightly mineral; that of the tomb is NNW and therefore soft.

He explained that each individual has his own "axis" which he called the "Baradat Axis" and so, after having worked over the silver reliquary busts of Saints Abdon and Sennen, he said that the bone relics in the tomb were those of Saint Abdon alone.

He concluded that once and for all, one must wipe out any idea that the tomb is supplied by any subterranean piping. One must also forget any idea of "atmospheric wells" or dew.

"This autonomous production of water" he said, "is in consequence, inexplicable and the mystery remains complete. As the natural law does not accept that water can spring from stone, one must conclude that it is miraculous, but there remain some tests and experiments to be done to check the last few points. Why hasn't the scientific world taken more interest in this phenomenon?"

Good question! But then who or what actually *is* the scientific world? Would you accept, for instance, the testimony of some French hydraulic engineers?

CHAPTER SIX

A SCIENTIFIC STUDY

In October 1958 a Mr "R.H.", an hydraulic engineer in Grenoble and two of his colleagues, asked the late Reverend Canon F. Dalqué, the then parish priest, for authority to make some scientific observations on the sarcophagus with a view to searching for the origin of the water. The priest accorded them every facility even, at one stage in 1961, giving them the keys to the gate of the small enclosure which lies inside the courtyard and which protects the tomb.

As a result, the scientists had total freedom for all their experiments and the parish priest had to put up with all their demands and their various comings and goings.

For two years, from January 1959 until December 1960, the review *"La Houille Blanche"* (Hydroelectric Power), 20, rue Rambaud, Grenoble, and now at 48, rue de la Procession, 75724 Paris Cedex 16, published a series of articles on the Holy Tomb, under the somewhat irreverent title of: "The Cult of the Water".

January 1959
In this first issue of that year, a certain Mr Delaunay Delapierre, a significant pseudonym which one thinks belongs to our Mr "R.H." and which translates as: Mr "Water born of stone", put the parameters of the problem of the sarcophagus to the readers under different headings:

Secret piping,
Inadvertant contact with a natural supply of water,
Clandestine filling,
Porosity of marble,
Rain-water,
Condensation.

With the aid of a sketch and a plan, he showed very fairly the complete absence of any secret piping and the impossibility of any inadvertant or clandestine filling.

Dealing with the hypothesis of condensation, he stated quite categorically:

"This can not be, for the temperature on the inside of the sarcophagus is two to three degrees higher than that of the outer casing itself; it is on this where the condensation should occur" (of the surrounding warm air). "But, apart from the small amount of humidity on the north-east vertical corner of the sarcophagus, the whole surface remains dry."

November 1959

This issue carried an article by a certain Mr Lapierre Devinoux another interesting pseudonym, which can be translated as: Mr "Stone, guess who we are"!

He said, in contradiction to the previous engineer, that condensation could nevertheless have an effect, and he quoted the example of the reservoirs of Theodosia which we have already covered in chapter five and to which we see no value in refering again.

To add to the documentary records of Mr Delaunay Delapierre, he quoted three other sources:

a) The notes of Mr Prosper Mérimée who visited Arles in his capacity of Inspector of Historic Monuments in about 1830 and who said humorously, that had Arnulfe emptied the wine, rather than the water into the tomb one would now have an inexhaustible supply of good wine. Local wines, however are not that bad!

b) The brochure published in 1954, in Perpignan, by Brother Pierre-Marie Orseolo of which he reproduced the passage where the monk clearly confirmed the miracle and finally,

c) An article by a Mr Dupasquier, in the Catholic review *"Ecclesia"* (October 1959 issue). Mr Dupasquier exposed at length in this article, but without accepting it himself, the theory of condensation of the water in the atmosphere. Mr Dupasquier is in fact in favour of the traditional Arlesian concept.

In sum, the November article by Mr Lapierre Devinoux, while putting before the readers of the review a number of various opinions, refrained from clearly expressing the personal opinion of the author himself.

December 1959

One saw the same with the article signed by a certain Nicolas Chtchpov. (Contact with the Russian Embassy in London, leads one to suppose that this is probably yet another pseudonym!) After having said that the atmospheric humidity is the only possible source of the water, he then gave several reasons which seemed to him, to put this hypothesis in doubt.

So at this stage, we have two engineers who disagree with each other and one who disagrees with himself!

1960

Another engineer from Grenoble who gave his name as Cyprien Leborgne (the one-eyed man!) reported, after analysis, that the tomb water was very pure, that the porosity of the marble was "practically nil" and that its density is 2.9.

In all these articles, the review is not able and does not seem to want to impose any clear cut conclusion on the reader of the true cause of the water. But things now change dramatically!

1961

In the January 1961 issue, *"La Houille Blanche"* informed us that three engineers were going to investigate the tomb at once and that they would publish their results as soon as possible in the magazine.

In December 1961 — ten months later — the magazine published the full report. Through the kindness of the present editor of *"La Houille Blanche"* I was given a photocopy of the complete 1961 report.

The report opened with a one-page curtain-raiser entitled "Miscellany" and was accompanied by a drawing of a bald-headed man wearing half-moon glasses and winking at his readers! One learns why as one reads on.

We were told that the curtain-raiser was written: "With the collaboration of Professor Cyprien Leborgne". This must be our Cyprien Leborgne who earlier on said that the stone of the coffin is impermeable.

The professor opened by saying that since the disappearance of his articles from the magazine, people might have thought that he had left for a well-earned retirement, but this was not the case. His articles had had to wait until the editor felt they deserved a space. The problem of the sarcophagus had not been forgotten and one could see proof of this in the following pages.

The professor first wished to thank publicly "Peppone and Don Camillo, for the understanding way with which he had been received and for all the facilities which they had put at his disposal." (One can guess who Don Camillo was but we are less sure about Peppone!)

The professor went on at great length, but hear him out in full, as this is the long awaited hydraulic engineering solution:

"The sarcophagus is in a locked enclosure and Monsieur le Curé was kind enough to place the key at our disposal so that we were able, at any moment of the day or night, during more than two months — with the sole exception of Easter week, due to the arrival of the faithful and tourists — to carry out our observations and experiments in accordance with our prepared plans.

"A bit late you will say — well yes! But try and understand me my dear friends: Arles sur Tech is a charming little town where the mimosa blooms in season, which spreads and grows languidly on the hills bathed in sunshine at the foot of the Pyrenees, which dispenses, at the height of summer some shade for its narrow streets. A calm little town where it does you good to do nothing but perhaps show the tourists the sarcophagus of Saints Abdon and Sennen before telling them of the virtues of the stone which produces the water.

"Yet we worked, cogitated, sounded, fingered, siphoned — and Heaven knows what else — and *horresco referens* — we put our finger on the drop which fills the sarcophagus.

"Now look at the problem facing our consciences.

"Under the slender vaults of the ancient cloisters, we explained to Monsieur le Curé, to Mr Rougé, (is this our 'Peppone'?) what we thought we had discovered . . . we know that the press is going to get hold of our researches, of our results, we also know that summer is approaching and that tourists will come. The editor's secretary is thinking, I am sure, of all the space in our magazine which he's going to have to give me for my next article . . . .

"Arles is a lovely little town, so welcoming, our new friends so charming . . . come on let's have a drink of malmsey at the Mourages wine cellar: Perard, (a junior colleague?) rough me out a report . . do you get my message? Take all the time you need and more — let a lot of water pass under the bridge — whatever happens we will have a lovely journey.

"That my friends is why your daughter has been silent for so long!"

The professor now spoils the scientific story a bit by telling us:

"When I say 'we' it was in fact the admirable and devoted Mr Rougé who, as a retired school teacher, put himself at our disposal, with all his kindness, his friendship, his patience, even his cartesian spirit, and who noted down each day at the same time, the readings of all our recording equipment. Who installed all the other equipment and everything which you will find in the following pages."

(I am only a translator here of the French text and not a literary critic but even so, this preface seems a very flowery and long-winded way of introducing what must have been a very awkward report to produce!)

At this point, it would have been mid-March 1961, the professor and his collaborator appear to have deserted "the admirable and devoted" Mr Rougé at Arles sur Tech to carry out all the experiments. Where the professor and his collaborator actually spent the next few months we are not told but it wasn't in Arles, for Mr Rougé sent his readings weekly to Grenoble so that the professor's young collaborator could write the report.

The next eight pages in the magazine contain the report which being signed "G.P.", suggests that it was probably written only by the collaborator, "Perard", and not the professor himself.

The first page has a caption, a caricature worthy of *"Punch"*, showing the parish priest and one of his desolated parishioners, scratching their heads while looking at the Holy Tomb which is spouting out all its water in large jets!

The first paragraph in italics briefly outlines the subject and ends with this sentence:

"One can draw off on average, three hundred litres a year."

This figure, which appears to be the thesis to be examined, is an unfortunate error for one has already seen evidence of 600 litres being drawn off in a quarter and the report itself also records, on its last page, that 600 litres were drawn off between June and December 1951!

Following this, the report described as "fantasies" the figures which were given to the researchers for the quantity of "water extracted" from the tomb, and call the earlier historical reports (quoted in chapters two and three): "deceitful experiments". A curious start for the professor's young collaborator!

Next one is told that "one to two litres of water collect each day" and that this water production takes place all the time and that it is a "constant phenomenon". At the end of the report G.P. says that this is not so!

The "team" say that when they went on site they installed around the tomb instruments to measure temperature, humidity, wind direction and force, water level in the tomb and rainfall.

The report now states that as it didn't rain for two months, the water level "did not move or rather it fell a *few* mms every time the parish priest drew off a *few* litres of water".

The engineers noted however, with pleasure, that the "few" at "least showed their recorders were working"!

We are then informed that the recording thermometer and the recording hydrometer gave some "beautiful curves" showing that it was hot near midday and that the humidity was highest near 6 a.m.!

The rain-water gauge didn't seem to have had a recording device fitted for our engineers said they used the official water board recordings which are sent to Paris.

It is to be noted that the nearest "official recordings" are taken at the entrance to the Spa Baths at Amélie les Bains. The baths are 200 feet closer to sea-level than the sarcophagus and the three miles, as a fit crow might fly, between the baths and Arles include two mountain spurs running from 600 to 1500 feet high! Thus the rainfall at the entrance to the Spa Baths in Amélie, can be totally different from that in the church courtyard in Arles!

The level of the water in the tomb was obtained, our engineers agree, by a very "rudimentary system". The tomb's own copper suction pump had a hollow plastic tube fixed to its spout and by placing a child's school ruler against the vertical hollow plastic tube "one could note, more or less, the variation in the level of the tomb's water".

Such a system, which was shown in a photograph in the magazine, could never give more than the vaguest indication of what was going on, for the upper end of the hollow measuring tube had no cover and so was open to the air and any falling rain!

Based on fifteen days worth of figures sent from Paris for the rainfall at the Spa Baths of Amélie les Bains and the early morning reading of the child's ruler by the retired teacher in Arles, the team said "It is difficult to make a valid comparison and to establish a perfect corelation between the rainfall graph and the level of water in the tomb."

I would agree with them 100%!

However nothing daunted and in spite of Professor Leborgne's earlier report, curiously repeated quite clearly yet again in this new report that the marble is impermeable, G.P.'s report concluded that the lid of the tomb, but not the rest of the body of the tomb, which is made of the same material, was permeable!! Further, it is recorded that the April rains took between three to six days to pass nearly a third of their volume into the tomb.

The young Perard however, fairly noted that the 8.2 mms of February '61 rain did not seem to have passed through the lid at all. I personally noticed that after an unusual "dry" in July '86, the rains of August and September '86, didn't pass through either so perhaps only certain special spring rains pass through!

An analysis of tomb water was made and had been published earlier by the professor but if any analyses of rain, tap or spring water were made, they were not published. Why risk spoiling a very amusing story!

The editor of *"La Houille Blanche"*, in reply to my recent request for the real names and full qualifications of all the engineers, was kind enough to say:

"I can find nothing concerning the identity of the authors!"

The exclamation mark is his, not mine.

After four reports, written by scientists using only pseudonyms and which reached no definite conclusions, and one amusing story where a professor's young colleague refutes his professor's findings and then further even contradicts himself, I turned to London for help.

Why not read their findings and then reach your own conclusion?

CHAPTER SEVEN

LABORATORY REPORTS BY "THAMES WATER"

Having now decided to call in a "second opinion" in the scientific world, I also decided to call up reinforcements and so got hold of my sister who lives in London.

She got in touch with Mr Bisset of Thames Water, who is the Quality Services Co-ordinator of the New River Head Laboratories, 177 Rosebery Avenue, London, EC1R 4TP. He wrote on 10 June '87:

"Further to our recent telephone conversation, please find enclosed two sample bottles. It will greatly assist our analysts if you could split the sample you have between the two bottles.

"I'm afraid that the analysis that we can perform will be limited by the age and volume of the sample. If a fresher sample becomes available, please contact me on the number above and I will be happy to supply futher bottles.

"Your case has sparked considerable interest amongst my staff and I would be grateful if you could supply any background details which you feel are relevant.

"Analysis and interpretation normally take three weeks from the date of receipt of a sample after which time I will contact you with our findings."

By pure luck I was in England that June and further I had a spare bottle of tomb water with me. My sister also had some of the tomb water at her home which I had sent her previously. Rather than wait until I could get a fresh supply from Arles in the laboratory bottles we sent these two samples to Mr Bisset.

We had his reply dated 11 September '87:

"I have pleasure in enclosing the analytical results for the two samples you submitted. Although I appreciate that such raw data is a little indigestable, it may help to expand the documented evidence available on the phenomenon.

"I have highlighted results from the first set of analyses which are almost certainly artifacts resulting from the use of a cold cream jar as a sample container. There is, for instance, an elevated level of zinc which probably relates to the fact that zinc oxide is a common constituent of cosmetic creams.

"If one excludes the spurious results, the similarity between the two sets of results is quite marked, indicating a constancy of source. The mineral composition of the samples is very low which, under normal circumstances, would lead one to conclude that the samples are either of rain-water or are derived from a very pure spring source.

"There are obvious limitations to ascertaining the origins of the water in a remote manner. Accepting these limitations, the most logical next step would be to look at:—

(a) A repeat sample from the sarcophagus
(b) A sample of rain-water from a collection vessel in reasonable proximity to the sarcophagus
(c) A sample from a nearby spring or stream
(d) A sample from a nearby cold water drinking tap.

Photographs of the sarcophagus would also be helpful."

In September four sets of sample bottles (without cold cream!) were sent out to Arles sur Tech, filled from the sources requested and sent back to the laboratories. The results were sent to us by Mr Bisset on 25 April 1988:

"Please accept my apologies for the long delay in my reply.

"I have enclosed the analytical results for the samples you submitted. The legend at the bottom of each sheet should allow you to identify the sample location.

"You will notice that yet again the sarcophagus sample had a very low mineral content, so low in fact that we can discount the possibility of the sample originating from either a tap or a local spring. Although the analytical results for the rain-water sample are more similar, my colleagues and I agree that even rain-water left to stand for a long period of time would not deteriorate in such a way as to give the same analytical profile as found in the sarcophagus sample.

"The only possibility, if we assume a natural origin, is that of condensation. Condensate is normally of a high purity but it is difficult to envisage a condensation mechanism yielding the type of volumes you have described.

"The only way forward for any further investigation would be by site measurements, e.g. rate of accumulation, temperature gradients, humidity etc. Unfortunately, this is slightly outside the scope of Thames, I'm afraid!

"Again, my apologies for the delay in replying to your enquiry, and many thanks for providing a pleasant diversion from our routine work. I wish you the best of luck should you decide to investigate further. If you do eventually find an explanation for this phenomenon, I would be grateful if you would let me know."

So we now have engineers responsible for the water supply of 11.5 million people. They have real names, real addresses, proper qualifications and the full backing of the New River Head Laboratories of London. These scientists say quite categorically, and I repeat their conclusion:

"The only possibility, *if we assume a natural origin*, is that of condensation. Condensate is normally of a high purity but it is difficult to envisage a condensation mechanism yielding the type of volumes you have described."

But if the origin is not natural but supernatural? Let's talk to a Theologian.

CHAPTER EIGHT

A THEOLOGIAN TALKS

I don't know if there has ever been a theological book written about the tomb but I know of a number of questions that have been put to one Theologian (The late Reverend Canon Barthas of Toulouse) who answered them thus:

Q. "Father, why are you so interested in this tomb?"

A. "Because I'm curious; this is an essential if you want to be well informed. This Holy Tomb is, to put it mildly, an exceptional curiosity. That which takes place inside this marble tank merits at the very least that a curious person looks to see if one can't find a cause, natural or not, which would explain its various aspects.

"Note that only a mind which is either very superficial or else is profoundly stubborn in its disbelief, can maintain that science has definitely swept away all notions of the supernatural or of miracles. Lourdes, in the middle of the last century, introduced one to the domain of scientific observation precisely at the moment when rationalism held forth that everything could be explained by natural causes. One can quote numerous cures which have been acknowledged as miraculous after the most rigorous of examinations by the leading lights of medical science and this has not yet come to an end, as the senior doctor of the Commission of Enquiry, Dr Olivieri has shown in his recent book: (*Are there still miracles at Lourdes?* Published in 1970, in French, by Lethielleux.)

"Anyway there are many other miracles than just simply cures. Certain well-known conversions are true wonders which only the intervention of divine grace can explain. There are, in the world of physics itself, some wonders which are inexplicable naturally and the water from the tomb is of this sort."

Q. "Do you know of other cases of water production due to tombs or relics of saints?"

A. "The whole world knows about what the Italians call the 'Manna

51

of Saint Nicholas'. The body of this Bishop of Myra (Asia Minor) is now to be found in Bari in Italy, where it has been since it was taken from the Muslims by a commando of the Italian navy and it produces water which, just like this tomb's water, is distributed to the sick.

"Or a more recent case: at the end of the 19th century, Charbel Maklouf a saintly hermit died in the Lebanon and his compatriots demanded that he be canonised. His body, perfectly preserved having all the aspects of life, emits a liquid abundantly which runs out between the thick side of his reinforced concrete tomb and one attributes to him numerous stunning miracles: (*Charbel Maklouf*, by Nasri Rizcallah, published in 1950 by Spes, Paris.)

"Mr Pierre Dumas, who was then the Director of the Toulouse newspaper *"La Victoire"*, assisted in 1950 at the opening of this tomb, which had been demanded through the Congregation of Rites, for the canonisation of this hermit. He also wrote his life story: (*Vie et prodiges du moine Charbel Maklouf*. Fatima-Editions, Toulouse, 1951, now out of print)."

Q. "Do you therefore approve of the declaration of the late head of the town's tourist office to the delegate from French TV in 1963, affirming his personal faith in the 'miracle' of the water?"

A. "I would be very much inclined to, for the engima of this water which renews itself without stopping, from the thickness of marble seems to me unsolvable without the intervention of the creative power of God. I have been present on numerous occasions on the feast day of the Saints, 30 July, and have seen forty to fifty litres of water drawn off and, the following day the level has been virtually the same. In the interval, no one has added water. How do you explain that? Only a pure atheist could say, but 'a priori', for he is certain that here there is no miracle, for one who forgets the Creator and the Master of the laws of Nature, these laws are totally intangible. However our wise men of today no longer dare to claim to be disciples of a Renan or a Zola.

"The denial of a miracle 'a priori' is so totally illogical that no sage (in the Sciences) ever stops there. The most audacious in their refusal of faith, for example like a Jean Rostand, take refuge in what they call agnosticism; that is to say that they refuse to want to look further than the forces of Nature. They forget that an agnostic is, etymologically speaking, a voluntary ignoramus, one who closes his eyes on the side of the Heavens."

Q. "Then you believe, that one day the Church will declare that this is a miracle?"

A. "For all these wonders which I call local, the Holy See leaves to the religious authorities of the country, the task of admiring and approving them if they don't lead to superstition. Rome will only intervene if there is a major interest in what it decides and judges for itself.

"But basically one already has approval in principal because since the beginning, the bishops have authorised the distribution and pious use of the water. There are numerous documents giving one the authority which reminds us and proves that since the 10th century, bishops and priests have held as perfectly legitimate the special respect in which one holds the water from the Holy Tomb.

"Monsignor Gerbet, who was one of the great minds of the last century, and who was Bishop of Perpignan from 1854 to 1864, spoke openly of the miracle of the Holy Tomb. He had meditated for a long time in the catacombs of Rome so as to write his beautiful book *Esquisse de Rome Chrétienne*. He was struck by the connection one could draw between the water from the Holy Tomb and that between the baptismal pool of the Pontian cemetry where the two martyrs were at first buried.

"Monsignor de Carsalade du Pont, half a century later, put his signature to a tract where we read: 'The sight of this marvellous water which does not dry up is an admirable thing. One could say a challenge to modern incredulity and a superb confirmation of the power of God who does what He pleases with the laws of Nature.' In 1910 he wrote an eulogistic preface to Canon Crastre's book in which he had proclaimed the miracle. The eminent prelate wrote: 'I have admired the care which you have taken to satisfy the requirements of the modern critic over the miracle of the Holy Tomb.'

"A message is not always understood by he to whom it is given; this is why the greatest of miracles can leave the greatest of minds indifferent. The freedom of man is such that two men equally intelligent and well informed, faced with an unquestionably established miracle, adopt different if not contradictory attitudes. Here are two examples:

"In 1892, the novelist Zola closely followed the medical findings of the healing at Lourdes of Marie Lebranchu; he even went as far as Rome declaring that he wanted to tell of a beautiful miracle in one of his novels. However, he set about writing a book which turned into open derision the cure of a bogus patient whom he called 'La Gavotte' and whom he described as looking exactly like Marie Lebranchu and who had the same illness. He carried the lie as far as having her die on her return to Paris. Catholics, infuriated by this pack of lies, proposed an open discussion with Zola in front of a jury. He refused obstinately and went as far as to offer Marie Lebranchu, who was poor, a handsome annuity for life if she would leave France. To those who persisted in asking him for a discussion of the case he replied: 'Even if I see all the sick cured at Lourdes, I will not believe in a miracle.'

E

"You can well understand that even if the Church, the Pope himself, had proclaimed the healing of Marie Lebranchu as miraculous, neither Zola, nor his admirers would have accepted this verdict.

"On the other hand, you may probably know of the case of Alexis Carrel. In 1903, he was a medical student and an unbeliever; he saw a miracle at Lourdes; he studied it closely and when he was convinced that this cure was inexplicable without the intervention of the Almighty, he made the case the subject of his thesis for his doctorate. The jury, unbelievers as was the mode at the time, refused to accept it. Loyally, he sacrificed the brilliant future which awaited him in France and exiled himself abroad (where he quickly became famous) to be able freely to express the faith which he had found through the miracle. In 1912, he won the Nobel Prize for Medicine."

Q. "One says from time to time: Put a roof over your tomb and you will see the miracle stop. Do you think that this solution would resolve the enigma?"

A. "An obstinate unbeliever won't change his ideas even if he is proved wrong. If the rain can no longer reach the tomb, they can still quote the humidity in the atmosphere, early morning dew etc. and finally their own obstinacy. Look again at Zola!

"An example from history will indicate to you that God can either put an end to or even lessen a miracle if one demonstrates a certain defiance towards Him. Since 1552, the body of Saint Francis Xavier had been miraculously preserved as if still living, in Goa (India). Two centuries later the Pope, wishing to verify the marvel personally, demanded that one should send him just the hand of the Missionary Saint. One obeyed. But the separated hand dried up and when I saw it it seemed to be 'mummified'. As for the body itself, it remained intact, but had lost its living aspect.

"But in effect a counter proof is done continually by means of all the ancient sarcophagi which one can see by the dozen in many places in the open air: Toulouse, Arles sur Rhône, Haute-Garonne etc. From all these monuments has anyone ever thought of drawing water? Why is the one which contains some relics, the only one which produces water on demand?"

Q. "For you then, what is God's object in ensuring a permanent supply of water in this tomb? One has heard a priest say that, as this water has no spiritual use, one can see no reason why God should perform a miracle here."

A. "The objection of that priest is based only on theory. God doesn't waive a principle of one of the laws He has established purely to excite our curiosity. But here, as at Lourdes, He gets us, by this water, to think of Him, to turn our thoughts to Him the forgotten one. It is here like an

55

anti-poison against modern atheism, the great illness of our time.

"A particularly striking example of the value of a miracle as a sign of a religious truth, is the feeding of the five thousand by Christ when, from the five loaves, there remained twelve baskets of uneaten bits. On the following day in the synagogue at Capharnaum, Jesus explained that the bodily food of the eve was the symbol of the spiritual food which would be His own body, destined, through the Eucharist, to feed the souls of the whole world."

Theology may be the answer but what does the ordinary mortal think? Let's read some of their letters:

CHAPTER NINE

WHAT DOES THE REST
OF THE WORLD THINK?

Numbers of letters are received here each year and the flux increases when a newspaper or the TV get interested. French TV ran a short programme on the tomb in 1964 and two newspapers have also talked about the "prize" of one thousand gold francs to be won by the first person to prove, without doubt, where the water comes from. Money always interests people!

"La Dépêche du Midi" a Toulouse newspaper, published an article on 29 July 1962 and the British magazine *"Weekend"* published a similar article on 2 September 1970. As both these articles included details of the prize-money, the "Reader Reaction" was very similar in both France and Great Britain! We were even sent a copy of the article in *"Weekend"* together with an anonymous solution from New Zealand!

It might prevent people wasting their time (and ours!) if a selection of the letters is given. Don't rush, the prize hasn't been won yet!

The 'Thousand Francs Prize' was instituted by the Revd Crastre who was Parish Priest at Arles sur Tech from 1909 to 1916. He believed firmly in the supernatural character of the water; "An act of continuing creation by God". He spelt this out in his book and I quote:

"This singular monument which God has touched with His hand is a permanent challenge to the disbelief of all the centuries and especially our own. It is the assurance, ever old and ever new, of the supernatural, denied in these days more than ever before and more than ever triumphant.

"In spite of what the rationalists, the would be intellectuals, physicists, chemists, doctors and others with their so-called scientific explanations, which they have difficulty believing themselves say, we, with an invincible conviction, say to them: *Digit Deus est hic!* The finger of God is here!"

It is thus up to candidates for the thousand gold francs, to show that it isn't and that there is a simple and natural explanation for the water in the tomb.

The local solicitor should be able to brief intending candidates of the exact rules but let's look first at a few of the unsuccessful letters.

Dr C. Van Nes — Holland   31 May 1964

"Dear Monsieur le Curé,
For some time the mystery of the water flowing from a closed tomb in the church of Arles has interested me a lot especially in my position as a para-psychologist.

Exactly two weeks ago on Whit-Sunday itself, I had the opportunity to visit Arles and to see the miraculous tomb. I didn't want to disturb you on that particular feast day, I'm the son of a university theologian, and so I only had the chance to talk about the subject with the Revd Paul Jaquem, Superior of "Notre-Dame des Grâces" in Toulouse.

As I wasn't able to return to Arles, I am writing this letter to you now that I am back in Holland. One is still looking for the origin of the water production, yet if it lies on a material plane, one would have found it long ago.

On the non-material plane, there are two possibilities:
1. It is a miracle of Heaven,
2. It is an 'occult phenomenon', if not demoniacal.
In the first case no one will be able to do anything about it.

In the second case, a person initiated in the secret sciences could bring a halt to the mysterious production of water, if not instantaneously, in any event after a certain lapse of time. An end to the production of the water will be the proof required that one found the true cause of the mystery.

I would be much obliged, dear Monsieur le Curé, if you would be kind enough to let me know, in due course:
1. If the water is still flowing at the rate of three litres a day, more or less,
2. If the production has diminished,
3. If it has ceased.
                              Yours faithfully,"

NB   Probably unnecessary to add that Mr Van Nes's occult influence has not been felt by the Holy Tomb!

A Radiesthesist's letter. — Tarn, France   2 August 1962

"Herewith my calculations as a radiesthesist: When the saints came into the area they discovered a spring of incorruptible water . . . . they used it for baptisms and cures. To keep up the good works the clergy buried the saints in the coffin and . . . ."

No, sir the saints never came here and they were buried in Rome!

Mr L. A. Johns — Kenton, Middlesex

"The tomb is in the sun all day (it isn't) and it has a number of cracks (it hasn't). The silicum, calcium and magnesium which the tomb contains (it doesn't) cause the water to collect."

No prize!

Mr Ch. Sch. — St. G. Lot, France   22 August 1962

"Is there an underground stream under the coffin.connected to it by pipes? Can one sound the walls and the floors? Is the effigy of the squire movable? I put these questions now before I come and see."

He never did!

Mr Breen — Hayes, Middx., UK   8 June 1970

"The article didn't mention the names of the two martyrs in the tomb from which one draws water. I think it must be Abdon and Sennen. I love these saints whom I invoked a few years ago when I was ill and I drank the tomb water to cure my illness.

I would be very grateful if you would send me a small container of the water."

No solution offered.

G.A.L. (aged 83.) — Toulouse, France   1962

"The sarcophagus is in constant communication, fortuitous or deliberate, with one of the numerous lakes in the neighbouring mountains or a spring whose level is slightly higher than the tomb which is filled by the well-known principle of water always finding its own level. The sarcophagus is just above an underground stream or lake and all that is necessary is to drill a hole to tap into it through the supporting legs or blocks."

This letter was accompanied by a sketch and the writer continued "Arles sur Tech is at the foot of the Canigou and is surrounded by other peaks. This proves my theory. It would be sufficient to drill a few holes around the tomb to find the hidden supply. An underground stream will be more difficult to find than a lake."

No prize. The coffin has been lifted up in the air in front of hundreds of witnesses and there are no pipes!

The anonymous reader in New Zealand.

"I have read that the foresters in the Sahara place a saucer cut in two at the feet of the trees. As the saucers have a groove cut in their edge they rest close to the tree trunk. A small hole is drilled in the saucer and the night's dew collects in the saucer and then drips onto the roots during the day."

We are still trying to work out how this ties in with a marble tomb in a stone-covered courtyard, devoid of trees!

Henriette P. — Toulouse, France   31 July 1962

"Dear Monsieur le Curé,
    Having spent all my youth in Perpignan I have often prayed in the abbey church of Arles.
    As for the problem of the arrival of the water, in essence this is unsolvable because it is miraculous. It is impossible to explain naturally the presence of the water in the Holy Tomb, because it has no origin nor spring on earth; all its secret comes from God!
    An analysis of this water, as for that at Lourdes, shows no natural virtues, neither preventitive nor curative and yet both are sovereign in the good they do, bringing real relief and miraculous cures to both bodies and souls . . .
    The miracle of the water at Lourdes came after the words and the ineffable smile of the Virgin to Bernadette. The water of the Tomb is entirely concentrated in the silence of God, it acts and reproduces itself to infinity by the power of God alone and His mysterious designs . . ."

No "natural" solution offered.

Miss Nellie Betts — England   18 June

"I think the marble has a tendency to remain humid through its contact with coal or sand which acts as a magnet to draw rain-water or other aquatic liquids. A small crack or hole probably lets the water in."

We stopped here as the writer believed the tomb to be buried deep underground!

Mr Campbell — Romford, Essex

"The solution to the problem lies probably in the fact that the tomb comes from Persia." (It doesn't.)

"In that country there grows a kind of plant which resembles our dandelion. It grows and flowers in deep shadow and one finds it often in tombs and caves. It is possible that some seeds got into the tomb there and have been growing inside for centuries. The flower produces a wet secretion."

No prize.

Mr Campbell however, also put the problem to the Geological Museum in London. They replied that they couldn't discuss the tomb without knowing more about it. They however joined our expert, mentioned in the prologue and also the Thames Water Engineers by concluding:

"It is unreasonable to think that atmospheric condensation can produce three gallons of water in a week from a tomb."

So what is the final answer?

CHAPTER TEN

CONCLUSION

I must say that I have been delighted and amazed at the enormous amount of recorded evidence that has been gathered over the last thousand years, on the subject of the "Holy Tomb".

Perhaps the mystery will never be solved but, I felt that, as a new local resident, I ought to make some sort of an effort of my own to add to the general store of information.

I count myself extremely fortunate to have been put in touch with Mr A. D. Bisset of the Thames Water Laboratory, who so kindly helped. To him and his staff and colleagues, I offer my grateful thanks. For those of you who understand water analysis, I have put his results at Annex "A".

What is one to think? Monks and priests furiously filling the tomb from tap or spring water which doesn't have the same chemical analysis? Secret pipes from secret reservoirs with the wrong sort of water? Rain-water that won't ever deteriorate into tomb water?

It must obviously be condensation. But this has been categorically denied by several scientists and any way this is where we came in!

Did I find out?
Yes I have for me. How about you!

In closing, can I remind you of Shakespeare's words spoken by "The noblest Roman of them all.":
"There are no tricks in plain and simple faith."

61

Annex "A" to *A Coffin of Clear Water*

Results forwarded by, Thames Water Laboratories London

Comparison of Results from Thames Water

| | | | | Water from: | |
		Tomb	Spring	Rain	Town
Date Tested		5/10/87	19/9/87	18/9/87	19/9/87
Determinand	Units	Result	Result	Result	Result
pH value		7.3	6.7	7.3	7.2
Conductivity at 20 C	usm/cm	158	223	43	155
Ammoniacal N as N	mg/l	0.150	0.017	0.130	0.014
T.O.N. as N	mg/l	2.7	4.7	0.5	0.3
Nitrite as N	mg/l	0.004	0.006	0.004	0.002
Chloride as CL	mg/l	5	6	5	5
Reac. Phosphorus as P	mg/l	0.58	0.23	0.04	0.04
Hardness as $CaCO_3$	mg/l	70	61	40	45
Alkalinity as $CaCO_3$	mg/l	38	40	0	44
Silica Reactive	mg/l	0.7	14.1	2.6	10.8
D. Copper	ug/l	10	10	10	10
Copper	ug/l	10	10	10	12
D. Zinc	ug/l	10	10	10	10
Zinc	ug/l	10	10	27	10
D. Manganese	ug/l	10	10	10	10
Tot. Manganese	ug/l	10	10	10	10
Iron Dissolved	ug/l	10	10	10	65
Irontotal	ug/l	10	10	144	161

Comparison of Results from Thames Water

		Water from: Tomb	Tomb
Date taken		15/3/87	16/7/87
Date tested		17/6/87	22/7/87
Determinand	Units	Result	Result
pH value		7.9	7.7
Conductivity at 20 C	usm/cm	157	150
Ammoniacal N as N	mg/l	0.047	0.010
T.O.N. as N	mg/l	30	2.2
Nitrite as N	mg/l	0.005	0.003
Chloride as CL	mg/l	5	0
Reac. Phosphorus as P	mg/l	0.05	0.08
Hardness as $CaCO_3$	mg/l	128	126
Alkalinity as $CaCO_3$	mg/l	58	48
Silica Reactive	mg/l	1.4	1.3
D. Copper	ug/l	10	10
Copper	ug/l	11	10
D. Zinc	ug/l	252*	10
Zinc	ug/l	276*	10
D. Manganese	ug/l	10	10
Tot. Manganese	ug/l	10	10
Iron Dissolved	ug/l	10	10
Irontotal	ug/l	10	23

* We got a rocket for using an old cold cream jar and we thought we had washed it properly!